lauren child

We honestly CAN look after your dog

Grosset & Dunlap

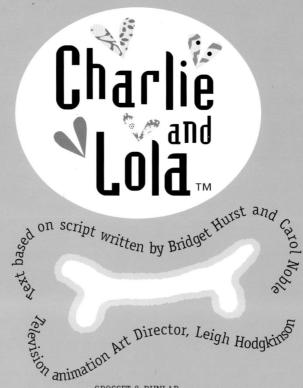

Charlie and Lola™

Text based on script written by Bridget Hurst and Carol Noble

Television animation Art Director, Leigh Hodgkinson

GROSSET & DUNLAP
Published by the Penguin Group
Penguin Group (USA) Inc., 375 Hudson Street, New York, New York 10014, U.S.A.
Penguin Group (Canada), 90 Eglinton Avenue East, Suite 700, Toronto, Ontario, Canada M4P 2Y3
(a division of Pearson Penguin Canada Inc.)
Penguin Books Ltd, 80 Strand, London WC2R 0RL, England
Penguin Ireland, 25 St Stephen's Green, Dublin 2, Ireland
(a division of Penguin Books Ltd)
Penguin Group (Australia), 250 Camberwell Road, Camberwell, Victoria 3124, Australia
(a division of Pearson Australia Group Pty Ltd)
Penguin Books India Pvt Ltd, 11 Community Centre, Panchsheel Park, New Delhi - 110 017, India
Penguin Group (NZ), Cnr Airborne and Rosedale Roads, Albany, Auckland 1310, New Zealand
(a division of Pearson New Zealand Ltd)
Penguin Books (South Africa) (Pty) Ltd, 24 Sturdee Avenue, Rosebank, Johannesburg 2196, South Africa

Penguin Books Ltd, Registered Offices:
80 Strand, London WC2R 0RL, England

Library of Congress Control Number: 2006004505

ISBN 0-448-44414-3   10 9 8 7 6 5 4 3 2 1

I have this little sister, Lola.
She is small and very funny.
At the moment Lola really, really wants to have a dog.
But Mum and Dad say she can't because our flat
is too small and Lola is too young to look after it.

Lola says,
"Say woof, Charlie."

So I say,
"Woof."

Then Lola says, "Sit!"

So I sit.

My
cereal
bowl
is
now

a dog bowl.

And she has made me a **dog** bed.

Lola just loves **dogs**.

A lot.

One day we went to the park.

There was me and my friend Marv,
Lola and her friend Lotta.
And Sizzles.
Sizzles is Marv's dog.

Lola loves Sizzles.

So does Lola's best friend, Lotta.

Lola says, "You ask."

Lotta says, "No you."

So Lola says,
"Marv, can we look after Sizzles?"

Marv says,
"Lola, do you know
about dogs?"

Lola says,
"Yes I do. Everything."

And Lotta says, "So do I."

Lola says,

"We know that Sizzles is a very extremely very clever dog.

And we know he can do really very good tricks."

Lotta says, "And if he wanted he could absolutely roll over."

Lola says, "And juggle. All sorts of things."

And **dance**.
    Definitely, I think.
Lotta, do you know
    I think
Sizzles
    can do
        really
            anything."

Lotta says,
    "And **paint pictures**.
And **speak English**."

Lola says,
    "And
        walk
            on
                two
                    legs.

Marv says, "Sizzles is the cleverest dog ever, anywhere. Watch this.

Sizzles. Sit, Sizzles! Sit!

Sit! Sit, Sizzles?"

While Marv is trying to
make Sizzles sit, I see some of our
friends playing soccer
and I think I'd really like to play, too.

So I say,
     "We could play just one game,
                    Marv."

Marv says,
     "But who is going to look after
Sizzles?"

     Lola says, "Me!"

          Lotta says, "Me!"

     I say,
"It's only for a little while.
          He'll be okay with Lola and Lotta.
          I'm pretty sure he will."

So Marv says,
"Okay.
But you do know
there are lots of **rules**
if you want to
look after Sizzles.

No **chocolates.**

No **cakes.**

And
no **sweets**
of **any** kind.

Completely no digging . . .

and

no chasing birds.

And

no splashing

in puddles.

And **definitely NO** taking **him** off the **leash.**"

Marv says,
"Do you honestly promise to
look after my dog?"

Lola says, "Honestly,
we do promise honestly,
to look after your dog."

Lotta says,
"Honestly and promisedly, we do,
to look after your dog."

Lola says,
"Dogs must be stroked and patted."

Lotta says,
"To tell them we're their friend."

Lola says,
"Playing is . . .
    what makes dogs happy."

Lotta says,
"And grooming makes dogs feel pretty."

Lola says,
    "Dogs must go outside
and must walk."

    Lotta says,
        "Otherwise what is the point
    of their legs?"

Then Lola says,
"Lotta, I don't think you really know
all about dogs like me."

And Lotta says,
"Lola, I really do know
everything about dogs."

Lola says, "But Lotta, I'm in charge."

And Lotta says,
"So am I."

Lola says,

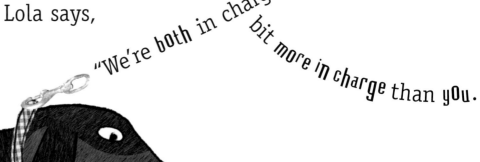

"We're both in charge, but I think that Mary said that I was a little bit more in charge than you.

"You see, Lotta, you must hold the leash like this. See?" Lotta says, "Oh no, Lola. Really you must do it like this."

"Ooops!"

"Sizzles, where are you?"

"Where are you, Sizzles?"

"Sizzles,
where
are
you?"

Lola says,
"Do you think we have
lost him **forever**?"

Lotta says,
"I think he was **sad** actually."

Then Lola says . . .

"Sizzles!"

But then Lola says,
    "Oh no! There are two Sizzleses!"

And Lotta says,
    "No, Lola, there are two dogs.
    But only one is Sizzles."

Lola says,
"But which one?"

Lotta says,
"I don't know."

Lola says,
"The clever one!
Sizzles can do anything, remember?"

Lotta says, "Yes. Sizzles can do anything."

Lola says, "Sizzles can sit!"

Then Lotta says,
"Sizzles! Sit. Sit. Sit!"

And Lola says,
"Sit. Sit. Sit!"

Lotta says,
"Sit, sit, sit,
sit!"

Then Lola says,
"Look! It must be Sizzles.
He's sitting!"

When me and Marv finished playing soccer,
we went to find Lola and Lotta.
I say, "Come on, you two. It's time to go."

But Lola and Lotta look a bit fidgety.

And they both whisper,
"Charlie, we had Sizzles
and we were
looking after him . . .

and then he sort of went for a walk . . .
without his leash.
And then we couldn't see him anymore.
And then we saw him but he wasn't one,
he was two Sizzleses.

And so . . . we're not sure

that Sizzles
is
Sizzles now."

So I say, "If you want to know what a dog's called, just look at the collar. See!
Dog number: 144. Sizzles.

Owner: Marv Lowe, 5a Crocodile Street."

Then Marv says,
"That's his dog tag. It's got his name and address on it, in case he gets lost.

All dogs have them."

And Lola says,
"We knew that actually, Marv."

And Lotta says,
"All dogs. Just in case
they get lost."

I say,
"Yes, that's right.
Just in case
they get
lost!"

And Lola says, "But Sizzles would **never** get lost."
Lotta says, "No, he's a **very extremely very clever dog.**"
Lola says, "He can do **anything.**"
And Lotta says, "He can do **absolutely anything.**"